W9-CBO-702

Go confidently in the direction of your dreams. Live the life you have imagined.
—Henry David Thoreau

Make sure your dreams for the future are non-negotiable.

Success lies in doing not what others consider to be great, but what you consider to be right.
—John Gray

I have a dream…
—Martin Luther King

Let us think of education as a means of developing our greatest abilities, because in each of us there is… a dream which, fulfilled, can be translated into benefits for everyone and greater strength for our nation.
—John F. Kennedy

When it comes to your dreams… don't let anything turn you around.
—Les Brown

Nothing can bring you peace… but yourself.
—Ralph Waldo Emerson

All that you accomplish or fail to accomplish with your life is the direct result of your thoughts.
—James Allen

*The Growing Field series was inspired by, and written in memory of, my colleague, mentor,
and friend Jason Dahl — the Captain of Flight 93 that crashed in Pennsylvania on September 11, 2001.
May your voice — and your leadership message — live on forever!*

*The Growing Field series is dedicated to my sister, Michele. You believed in me and this series long before I did...
with a world of love and thanks.*

*Dream Machine is dedicated to my three spectacular dreamers: Branson, Morgan, and Mitchell.
Having children like you is what dreams are made of. I love you guys — you rock!*

*For Mom and Dad: Thank you for teaching me to dream.
There was a magical place I knew growing up where anything was possible...
It was a special place the two of you made that I was lucky to call "home."
You have my eternal love and gratitude — for everything!*

*As always for my wife, Kristi — God only knows where I would be without your belief in me.
Your unconditional love and friendship has helped me to dream again.*

— Mark Hoog

*To Bob Aukerman, my father and best friend. Thanks for teaching me to dream big, work hard, and play even harder.
Special thanks to my assistant illustrator, Will Roth, for his creative and artistic contributions.
Your hard work has made the twists and turns of the illustrative roller coaster much smoother.*

*Heartfelt thanks to the following friends for their artistic help and support:
Leila Singleton • Tasica Singleton • Jeff Roth • Randy Pfizenmaier • Thalia Stevenson*

— Rob Aukerman

A portion of all Growing Field proceeds are donated to the Children's Leadership Institute for the promotion of youth character education.
A portion of all Growing Field proceeds are donated to the Jason Dahl Scholarship Fund.

Text and illustrations copyright © 2007 by Growing Field Books.
The Growing Field imprint and characters are a Growing Field International trademark. All rights reserved.

This is a work of fiction. All names, characters, places, or incidents are the product of the author's imagination or are used fictitiously, and any resemblance to actual persons, living or dead, events, or locales is entirely coincidental.

No part of this publication may be reproduced or transmitted in any form or by any means, electronic or mechanical, including photocopying, recording, or by any information storage and retrieval system, now known or to be invented, without permission in writing from Growing Field Books.

For information regarding permissions, contact Growing Field Books at:

Growing Field Books
2012 Pacific Court,
Fort Collins, Colorado 80501
or through: info@growingfield.com

Written by Mark E. Hoog. Illustrated by Robert J. Aukerman.
Designed by Lisa Conner and Zeto Creative. Edited by Jennifer Thomas of Beyond Words Editing.

Publisher's Cataloging-in-Publication
(Provided by Quality Books, Inc.)

Dream Machine: A Growing Field Adventure/ by Mark E. Hoog; illustrations by Robert J. Aukerman.

SUMMARY:
In the Growing Field carnival, three young children learn that they hold the key to their dreams
and their own dream machine.

Library of Congress Control Number: 2006926823
ISBN-13: 978-0-9770391-1-1
ISBN-10: 0-9770391-1-0

1. Self-esteem--Juvenile fiction.
2. Self-efficacy--Juvenile fiction.
3. Goal (Psychology--Juvenile fiction.
[1. Self-esteem--Fiction. 2. Goal (Psychology)—Fiction.]
I. Aukerman, Robert J.   II. Title.

PZ7.H76335Dre 2007
[Fic]
QBI06-600196

2nd Printing, March 2010. Printed in China.

Growing Field Books
Where children go to grow!

"Mark Hoog's book delivers an important message to young readers: If a dream is worth having, it's worth working for. If you believe in yourself and are dedicated to achieving your goals, you can accomplish anything— all it takes is hard work and determination. I encourage you to follow the example of the children in Dream Machine *and make your dreams come true."*

—William Jefferson Clinton
42nd President of the United States of America

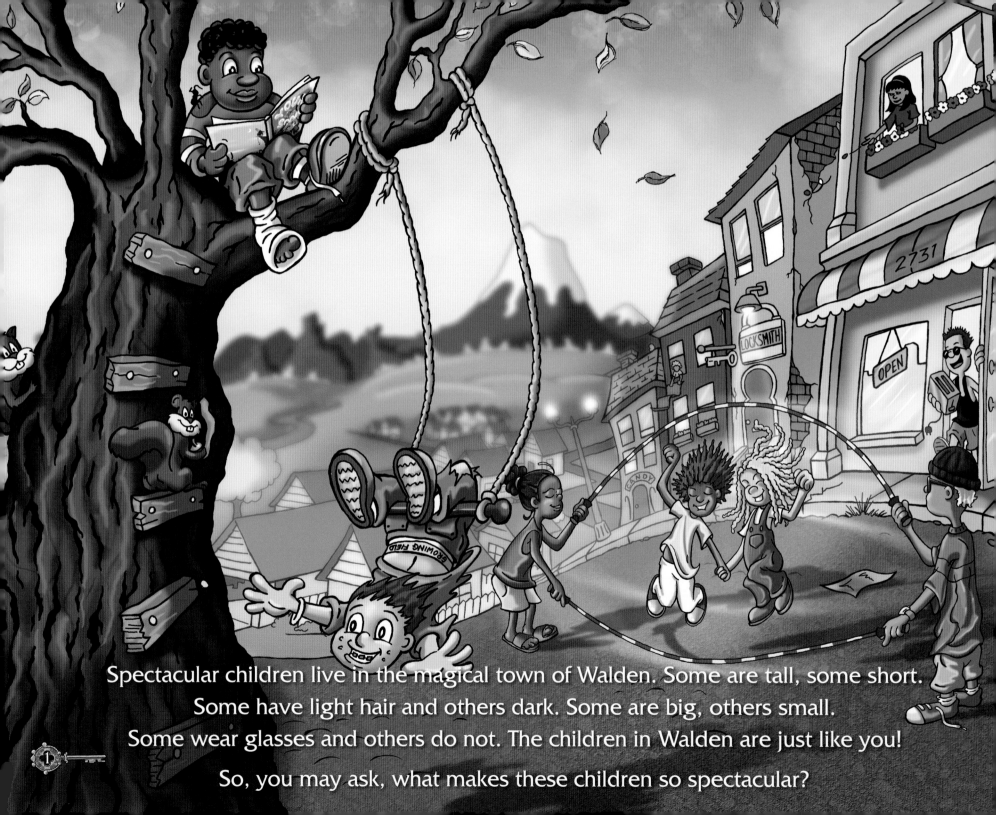

Spectacular children live in the magical town of Walden. Some are tall, some short.
Some have light hair and others dark. Some are big, others small.
Some wear glasses and others do not. The children in Walden are just like you!

So, you may ask, what makes these children so spectacular?

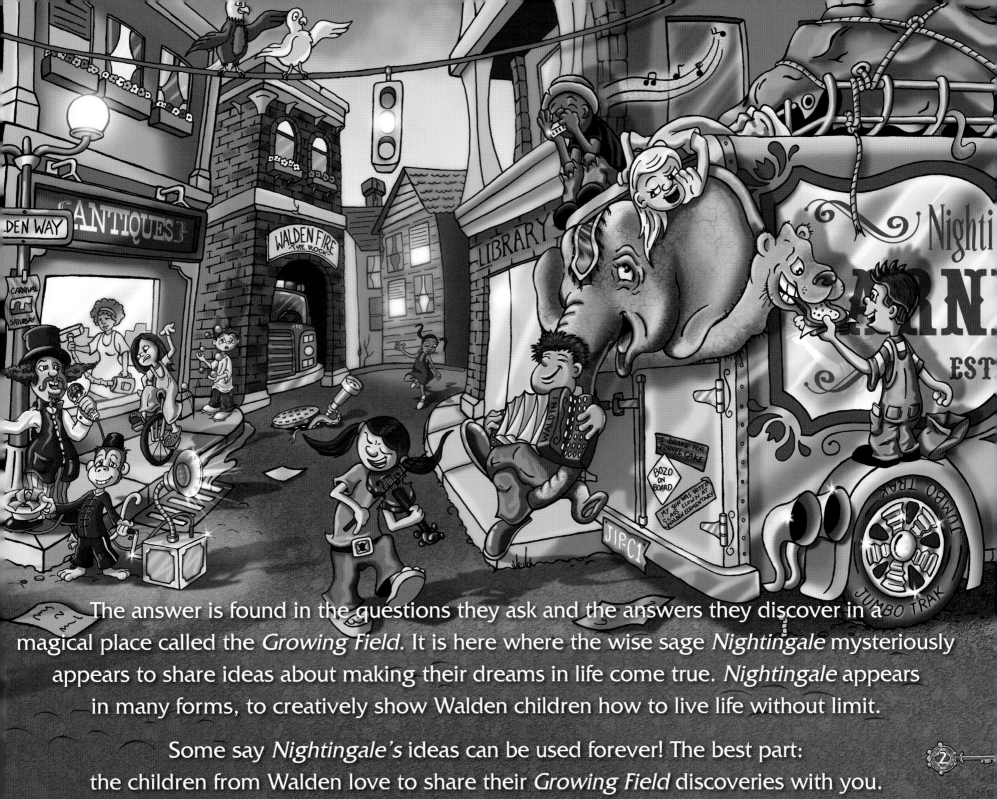

The answer is found in the questions they ask and the answers they discover in a magical place called the *Growing Field*. It is here where the wise sage *Nightingale* mysteriously appears to share ideas about making their dreams in life come true. *Nightingale* appears in many forms, to creatively show Walden children how to live life without limit.

Some say *Nightingale's* ideas can be used forever! The best part: the children from Walden love to share their *Growing Field* discoveries with you.

Today was another special day in Walden as Jazzmin, Bernquist, and Jackson walked home together from school. As they made their way through their usual shortcut, they noticed something shining through the dirt.

Jazzmin picked up the unknown treasure and blew away the dust. "Look what is written on the side!" she exclaimed. Today she just had to ask…

"What if there was a machine that could make our dreams come true?"

Suddenly, from nowhere, came a voice loud and clear.
"Step right up!" the voice bellowed. "Get your wish granted here!"

A carnival gypsy appeared on the scene, clothes draped all around her and hair neon green.
Long crazy eyelashes in spider-like loops, and ears that sparkled with huge golden hoops.
A flowing bandanna hung from her head to the floor.
"Somewhere," thought Jazzmin, "I've seen this woman before."

"Step right up!" the gypsy continued to holler.
"Get your wish here, tonight…one wish for one dollar.
Nightingale's Dream Machine will make dreams come true.
Take my hands, close your eyes—this adventure's for you."

6

The dust started to swirl as a gentle breeze blew,
and in front of their eyes a carnival grew. There were prizes and candy
and games to be played. The three just stood quietly...completely amazed.
A tent in the distance soon caught their eyes, as from it a light reached into the sky.

8

An incredible sight—this canvas stretched tight!
What was inside that was shining so bright? Glowing so strong nothing else could be seen,
but yellow, and purple, and red, orange, and green. From the top of the tent,
in the sky words were shown…words that to children are now clearly known.

Reaching the light, in half each child bent;
their faces peeked under the side of the tent.
And then, filled with excitement…inside each one went.

Standing and gaping—looking once and then twice—
each stared in amazement at a crazy device.

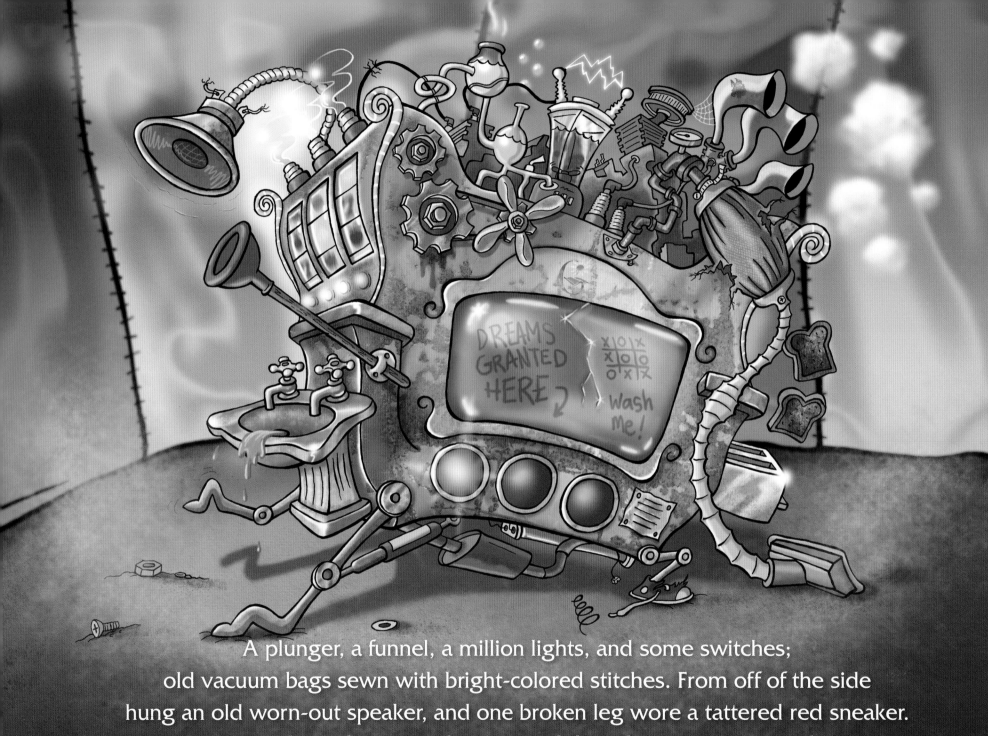

A plunger, a funnel, a million lights, and some switches;
old vacuum bags sewn with bright-colored stitches. From off of the side
hung an old worn-out speaker, and one broken leg wore a tattered red sneaker.
Levers and toggles, some buttons and thread; on it, some words...
could they believe what it said?

Through the Dream Machine, *Nightingale* started to speak.
The machine smoked and hissed; it creaked, and it leaked.

"You'll each press a button and let your dreams flow. Speak into this microphone,
so your dreams I can know. Who wants to go first? Your dreams must be specific.
Each will be given, so think: What would make *your* life terrific?"

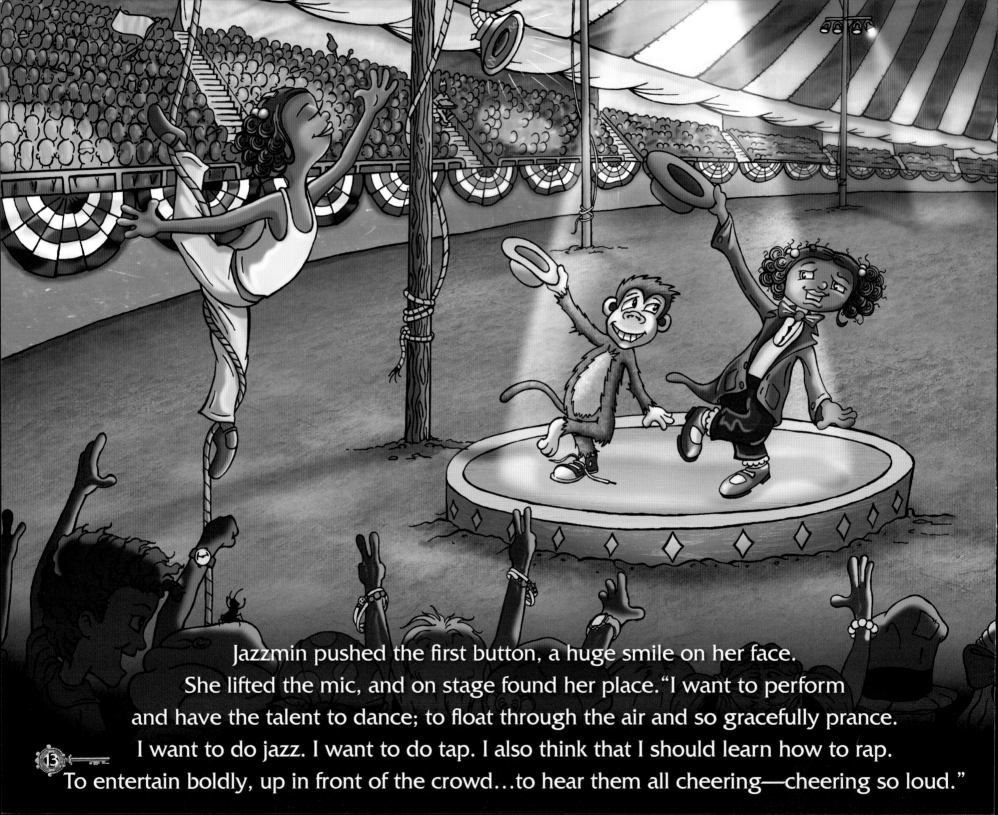

Jazzmin pushed the first button, a huge smile on her face.
She lifted the mic, and on stage found her place. "I want to perform
and have the talent to dance; to float through the air and so gracefully prance.
I want to do jazz. I want to do tap. I also think that I should learn how to rap.
To entertain boldly, up in front of the crowd…to hear them all cheering—cheering so loud."

Flashing lights and a siren, some wind and some smoke—
Nightingale listened and through the Dream Machine spoke:
"Your dreams I have heard, so now on with the show.
Let me hear from the others; their dreams, too, I must know."

Pushing his button, Bernquist yelled: "I want to fly! All that's extreme is what I will try. I'll jump on my bike and flip in the air, and do radical things that others don't dare. To ski and to ride, and even to skate; to board and to surf—all seem my fate. These are my dreams and I have no fear. I thank you, *Nightingale,* for bringing them near."

"Your dreams will come true," promised *Nightingale*. "Your dreams will be cast.
And now let's continue; let me hear the last."

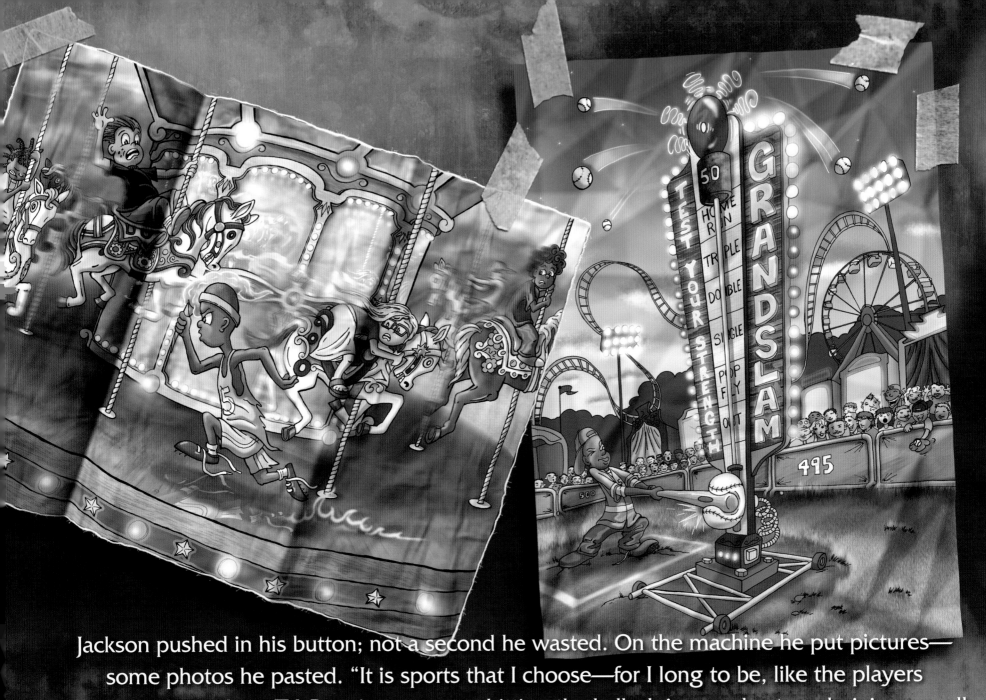

Jackson pushed in his button; not a second he wasted. On the machine he put pictures—some photos he pasted. "It is sports that I choose—for I long to be, like the players I watch each week on TV. Running my race, hitting the ball, doing my best, and giving my all. I want to be an athlete at the top of my game, a role model for others headed for fame—with a cereal box that shows clearly my name."

"All your dreams shall be granted," *Nightingale* now spoke.
The machine hissed one big "Sssss" and let out more smoke.

With all the dreams told, the Dream Machine they'd now test.
But to this day in Walden…no one believes what happened next.

Nothing. No rumble. No rattle. No ring.
The Dream Machine did nothing. It did not a thing.
No whistles. No sirens. No buzzers or lights.
The smoke that once hissed was now nowhere in sight.

"How can this be?" Jazzmin asked.
"Is this Dream Machine broke?" She then had an idea,
and of it she spoke:

"This machine needs our help, and fix it we must.
Let's replace every toggle and brush off the dust;
we'll clean every gear and remove all the rust."

With some tools and some time,
they did all they could do. Soon, the once-tired
Dream Machine looked better than new.
But was it enough?
Could their dreams now come true?

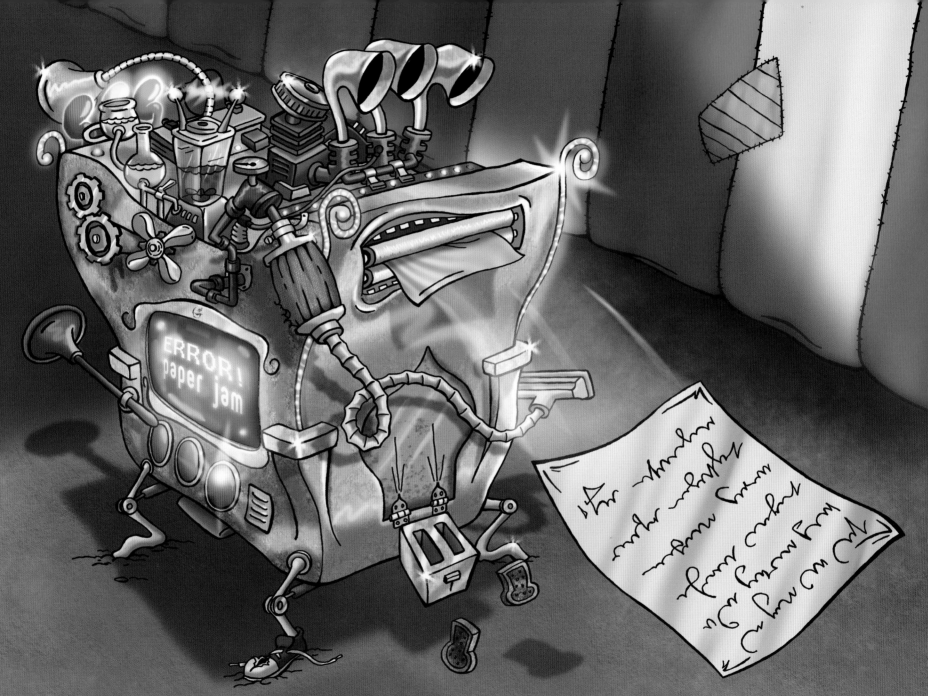

A faint noise emerged from one tiny slot. The machine spit one piece of paper…
then a whirlwind it shot. A rainbow of sheets flew and fell to the ground.
"Instructions," said Jazzmin, "are what we've just found."

"Work hard for your dreams," Jazzmin read. "Put YOURSELF on the stage. The price is hard work, which by you must be paid."

"It all starts right now," read Bernquist. "How you choose to start running. What you want for tomorrow you TODAY must start becoming. You will surf, skate, and fly—a certain event! Your price is your practice, the time that you've spent."

"Each of your dreams," Jackson read, "waits to come true. Talk of your dreams and what you're willing to do. And a cereal box photo for all to behold, will reflect what you've dreamed— that's the tale to be told!"

Nightingale's message delivered so well. Each dreamer now had one more story to tell.

"I'll practice," said Jackson, "day after day. My dreams will come true; my heart I'll obey."

Jazzmin was confident of all she would do.
"Instead of wishing, I'll start *doing*. My dreams will come true."

Bernquist proclaimed just how hard he would strive: "I will train and never quit,
to keep my dreams alive. I will work harder than anyone…my own special quest.
I'll capture my dreams on my own—I think that would be best."

Without any warning, to life the Dream Machine sprang. The lights all lit up
and the buzzers all rang. The whistles all whistled; each spring suddenly sprung.
Smoke filled the air. Their dreams had begun!

The commotion finally calmed; the air began to clear.
Then, all at once, a magical sight did appear. From out of a funnel,
small Dream Machines came. One for each dreamer—each marked with a name.

Nightingale," Jazzmin murmured, "there's just one thing we don't know: What is the magic that made your Dream Machine go? Perhaps the inside to us you could show."

"I'm sorry," explained *Nightingale*. "Inside no one can see. Not until one special girl can find one magic key."

Jazzmin smiled, knowing *she* held the key to unlock it. She reached her hand down, deep into her pocket. "We found this outside," she said, presenting the key. "Now let's open these doors…for the whole world to see!"

25

What would be the magic that filled each dreamer with hope?
A motor? A pump? Perhaps some pulleys with rope?

Each dreamer was aware that if the secret they knew,
their dreams could take flight and all could come true.

With a push and a pull and a turn of her wrist, Jazzmin unlocked the lock
with one simple twist. Bernquist removed it with one final tweak.
Jackson pulled open the doors, and *Nightingale* began softly to speak.

"Tonight you have learned how to make your dreams grow.
The key is the dreamer—this you now know. Dreams are for those who come up with a plan,
who believe in themselves and believe that they can."

"What is the magic that makes dreams come true? You can now share with the world…"

Jazzmin, Bernquist, and Jackson opened their eyes to see their mother standing
across the dusty lot, her golden hoop earrings sparkling in the sun.
They rushed to show her their carnival prizes.

Excited to return to Walden and share their *Growing Field* adventure with friends,
the three first opened their Dream Machines. Each contained a special note:

You hold the key to your very own

Dream Machine. I look forward

to watching you work to make all

your dreams in life come true.

I love you, little dreamer.

Nightingale

Discussion Seeds for DREAM MACHINE

Through the first Growing Field adventure, Your Song, we helped our children discover their unique gifts and talents. Now let's help them develop those skills by learning to become excellent dreamers.

Goals are simply dreams with deadlines. Help your child understand that dreams and goals for the future turn the "Impossible" into the "I'm possible."

To help your child become a spectacular dreamer, encourage him or her to:

- Identify and verbalize dreams
- Write and visualize goals for the future
- Work every day in pursuit of personal goals

It is up to us to believe in our children—and their dreams—as they learn to believe in themselves. Let your child know that life is without limit, and that it all begins with a dream.

Today is a great day to help your child learn to use his or her own Dream Machine.

Dream big with your child today!

This personal growth and leadership book belongs to:

_____

My dreams list:

_____

_____

_____

_____

Welcome to the Growing Field!

Read what leaders are saying about their magical journey through the Growing Field…

"Mark Hoog's book delivers an important message to young readers: If a dream is worth having, it's worth working for. If you believe in yourself and are dedicated to achieving your goals, you can accomplish anything—all it takes is hard work and determination. I encourage you to follow the example of the children in *Dream Machine* and make your dreams come true."

—William Jefferson Clinton, 42nd President of the United States of America

"A walk through Mark Hoog's Growing Field series is a wonderful and creative way for any adult to help grow a child's self-esteem, character, and love of reading. Everyone can benefit from the seeds to be found in the Growing Field."

—Richard Riley, U.S. Secretary of Education

"Mark Hoog is doing the most important work in America today—growing our children. With Magic and Treasure and Dreams and Songs and Gifts, he's helping them learn to lead. Mark's work is one of the best gifts you can give both children and adults. The Growing Field series MUST be the next thing you read and share with others."

—W. Mitchell, Top Motivational Speaker U.S./Australia

The Seeds of the Growing Field…

Following the events of 9-11, including the death of his close friend and colleague, Jason Dahl—Captain of Flight 93, which crashed in Pennsylvania—author Mark Hoog struggled to find meaning and purpose in a challenging time.

In Hoog's darkest moment, powerful thoughts from his past literary readings—everything from Aristotle to Thoreau to Confucius to Tony Robbins—presented themselves to him in the form of simple bedtime stories for children. Each story delivered ideas associated with some of our greatest leaders and philosophers, at a level simple enough to introduce children to the concepts of personal growth and leadership. The Growing Field series was born.

Today, the Growing Field series is enjoyed around the world and is recognized for its motivational and inspirational message to youth. The Growing Field serves to let children know we believe in their life—and reminds adults that it is never too early to teach our children the ideas and behaviors associated with living life without limit!

Growing Field Books
Where children go to grow!

Seeds of Success are found in the Growing Field

Children of all ages will delight in learning valuable life skills from the nationally acclaimed Growing Field personal growth and leadership book series.

The Growing Field introduces children to ideas and beliefs that will enable them to **_Live Life without Limit!_**

Plant Seeds of Success in your child today!

Collect the entire Growing Field leadership series!

Your Song introduces children to their unique gifts and talents.

Dream Machine invites children to dream about their possibilities.

Field of Dreams teaches children to cultivate the "Seeds of Success" planted by their dreams.

ORDER at WWW.GROWINGFIELD.COM OR anywhere fine books are SOLD! TOLL-free 1-866-465-4211

WOW!

JACKSONBII5

Yes, I am a dreamer. For a dreamer is one who can find his way by moonlight, and see the dawn before the rest of the world.
— Oscar Wilde

There is always one thing you can do when the pressure pushes in on you. Dream bigger!

You create your opportunities... by asking for them.
—Patty Hansen

You will become what you think about most.

Happy are those who dream dreams and are ready to pay the price to make them come true.
—Leon J. Suenes

Children have more need of models than of critics.
—Joseph Joubert

You can't just sit there and wait for people to give you that golden dream. You've got to get out there and make it happen for yourself.
—Diana Ross

You've got to have a dream. If you don't have a dream, how will you make a dream come true?
— Blaine Lee